There Doesn't Have to be a Reason

by MC Kasper

FLARE KIDS, an imprint of Catalyst Press, El Paso, Texas

There Doesn't Have to Be a Reason

Copyright © 2024 M. C. Kasper

All rights reserved.
No portion of this book may be reproduced
in any form without permission from the publisher,
except as permitted by U.S. copyright law.

For further information, write info@catalystpress.org
In North America, this book is distributed by
Consortium Book Sales & Distribution, a division of Ingram.
Phone: 612/746-2600
cbsdinfo@ingramcontent.com
www.cbsd.com
In South Africa,
this book is distributed by Protea Distribution.
For information, email orders@proteadistribution.co.za.

ISBNs: Print 978-1-963511-10-9, Ebook 978-1-963511-11-6

FIRST EDITION
10 9 8 7 6 5 4 3 2 1

Library of Congress Control Number: 2024942204

There Doesn't Have to be a Reason

"But can your tail help you swim?" asked the beaver.
"Let's see!"

"Yeah, I'll stick to using my paws to swim instead of my tail."

"Can you hold things with your tail?" asked the opossum.

"Does this count?"

"Then no, my tail can't grab things.
But my paws are excellent at it."

"Can your tail help you when you are flying?" asked the bird.

"Can you detatch your tail so you won't get eaten?" asked the Skink.

"No, but then again the idea never ocurred to me to try."

"Nope, it's stuck on good."

"Good thing I don't need my tail to balance, because that did not work out."

"Can your tail help keep bugs off you?" asked the bison.

"No, but I wish it could."

buzz... buzz... buzz...

"Can your tail help scare animals away?" asked the rattlesnake.

"Is it gone? Since wagging my tail doesn't make noise, I think I'll just stick to climbing trees or making myself look bigger."

"Can your tail help you communicate?" asked the wolf.

"See? We wag when we're happy and we puff our tails up when we're mad."

"Why do you like your tail so much then?" asked the squirrel.

"Yea, it can't even help you out," said the bison.

"I don't understand. Why does something have to be useful to be liked?" asked the bear.

"My tail may not serve a big purpose, like all of yours, but it's mine and I love it. There doesn't have to be a reason."

"Plus it keeps my bear bottom warm."

*Special thanks to all those
who helped make a dream reality
and being a never ending soundboard
and source of support.*